D1505444

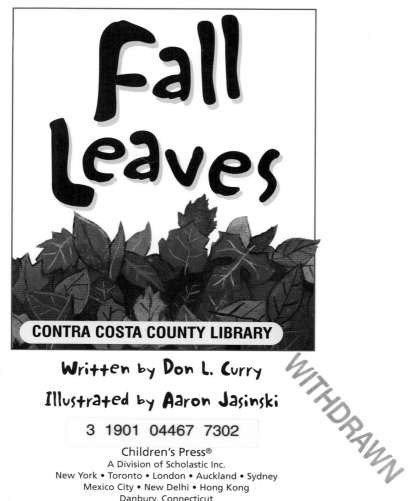

**CONTRA COSTA COUNTY LIBRARY**

Written by Don L. Curry

Illustrated by Aaron Jasinski

Children's Press®
A Division of Scholastic Inc.
New York • Toronto • London • Auckland • Sydney
Mexico City • New Delhi • Hong Kong
Danbury, Connecticut

To Mrs. Miracle...my first grade teacher
—D.L.C.

To my family
—A.J.

Reading Consultants
**Linda Cornwell**
Literacy Specialist

**Katharine A. Kane**
Education Consultant
(Retired, San Diego County Office of Education
and San Diego State University)

Library of Congress Cataloging-in-Publication Data
Curry, Don L.
    Fall leaves / written by Don L. Curry ; illustrated by Aaron Jasinski.
        p. cm. – (A Rookie reader)
    Summary: A child describes all the fun to be had with fallen leaves.
    ISBN 0-516-25904-0 (lib. bdg.)        0-516-26831-7 (pbk.)
    [1. Leaves–Fiction. 2. Play–Fiction.]  I. Jasinski, Aaron, ill. II. Title. III. Series.
PZ7.C93595Fal 2004
[E]–dc22                                    2003018615

6 7 8 9 10 11 12 R 14 13 12 11 10 09 08            62

I rake the leaves.

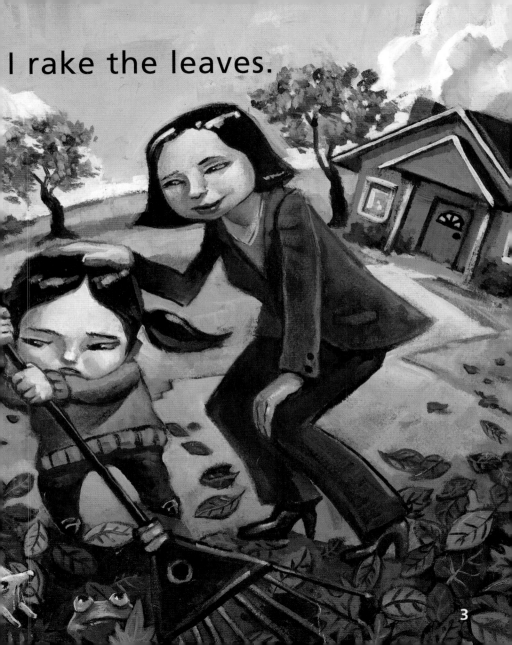

I pile up the leaves.

I jump in the leaves.

I roll in the leaves.

I throw the leaves.

I hide in the leaves.

I dig in the leaves.

I dance in the leaves.

I spin in the leaves.

I rake the leaves.

We jump in the leaves.

# Word List (15 words)

| | | |
|---|---|---|
| dance | jump | spin |
| dig | leaves | the |
| hide | pile | throw |
| I | rake | up |
| in | roll | we |

## About the Author

Don L. Curry is a writer, editor, and educational consultant who lives and works in New York City. When he is not writing, Don can generally be found in the park reading, or exploring the streets of the greatest city on Earth, on his bike.

## About the Illustrator

Aaron lives in the Seattle area with his wife, where he works as an illustrator. He likes root beer and hopes to someday bowl a perfect 300 game. He always enjoys painting new and exciting subjects.